For Charlie, my very best helper
—A.S.

To my friends—thanks for looking out for me.
—T.M-W.

Text copyright © 2019 by Annie Silvestro
Jacket art and interior illustrations copyright © 2019 by Tatjana Mai-Wyss
All rights reserved. Published in the United States by Doubleday,
an imprint of Random House Children's Books,
a division of Penguin Random House LLC, New York.

Doubleday and the colophon are registered trademarks of Penguin Random House LLC.

Visit us on the Web! rhcbooks.com
Educators and librarians, for a variety of teaching tools,
visit us at RHTeachersLibrarians.com

Library of Congress Cataloging-in-Publication Data
Names: Silvestro, Annie, author. | Mai-Wyss, Tatjana, illustrator.
Title: Bunny's Book Club goes to school / by Annie Silvestro ; illustrated by Tatjana Mai-Wyss.
Description: First edition. | New York : Doubleday, [2019]
Summary: Bunny's human friend, Josie, is nervous about starting a new school so he and
his Book Club friends pay her a surprise visit—once they get past the distractions.
Identifiers: LCCN 2018018471 (print) | LCCN 2018024281 (ebook)
ISBN 978-0-525-64464-4 (hc) | ISBN 978-0-525-64465-1 (glb) | ISBN 978-0-525-64466-8 (ebook)
Subjects: | CYAC: Schools—Fiction. | Friendship—Fiction. | Books and reading—Fiction. | Animals—Fiction.
Classification: LCC PZ7.1.S545 (ebook) | LCC PZ7.1.S545 By 2019 (print) | DDC [E]—dc23

Book design by Martha Rago
MANUFACTURED IN CHINA
10 9 8 7 6 5 4 3 2 1

First Edition

Annie Silvestro

Bunny's Book Club
GOES TO SCHOOL

Illustrated by Tatjana Mai-Wyss

Doubleday Books for Young Readers

Bunny's Book Club met at the library every Saturday.
Bunny and his forest friends arrived even before the
librarian. They couldn't wait to return the books they had
borrowed and to pick out new ones.

They always found lots to do at the library.

Porcupine had discovered arts and crafts, and Bird loved the audiobooks. Raccoon typed at a computer, while Bear and Mouse nosed through cookbooks and Frog put puzzles together. Squirrel searched the highest shelves as Mole mined below.

And Bunny, well, Bunny had made a new book buddy. A little girl named Josie also came to the library every Saturday. She recommended books to Bunny. And helped him with the hard words.

Bunny loved Josie almost as much as he loved books. His friends loved her, too.

One crisp-cool day, Josie slumped down onto the pillow pile beside Bunny.

"I start my new school next week," she said.

Bunny's ears perked up. He had read all about school!

"I'm so nervous," she continued. "What if I don't make any friends?"

"Who wouldn't want to be your friend?" sputtered Bunny.

Bunny hated to see Josie worry. He wanted to help. But how?

That night, as he hopped into bed, an idea popped into his head:

Josie needed a friend.

Bunny *was* a friend.

That was it!

Monday morning, Bunny bounced out the door . . . and right into Porcupine.

"Where are you off to?" Porcupine asked.

"School," said Bunny. "It's Josie's first day and she needs a friend."

"I'm her friend," said Porcupine. "I'll come, too."

"I suppose two friends are better than one," said Bunny.

So off they went.

Along the way, they bumped into Bear.

"We're going to school," said Porcupine. "Wanna come?"

"Oh, brother," said Bunny.

"Don't get your whiskers in a twist," said Porcupine.

"Three friends are better than two!"

But then three friends turned into four.

Then five.

Then six, seven, eight, and nine.

When their crew reached the town, Bunny came to a halt. School was bigger than he'd thought. He scanned the crowd and shook his head.

"No way we're gonna find her," he said.

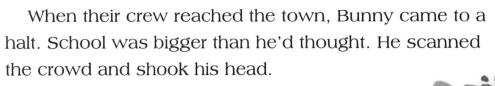

Then, as the last of the students swarmed inside, Bunny spotted Josie.

"There she is," he called. "Let's go!"
The animals quickly darted after her. But by the time
they reached the door, Josie was gone.

They peeked into classroom
after classroom.
"That's her!" said Squirrel.

Everyone tumbled into the gymnasium.
But it wasn't Josie.

A ball whizzed over their heads.

They couldn't resist jumping and dodging and dunking . . .

until Bunny blew a whistle.

"We have a job to do," he said. "Come on!"

The animals hurried out. Except for Squirrel.

"I'm gonna hang out here just another minute," she said.

A song floated down the hall. Bird followed the notes.
"I think it's Josie!" she trilled in tune. And she fluttered
into the music room.

But it was another false alarm.

"I'll stay to help with the harmony for a bit," said Bird.

Just then, a delicious smell wafted through the air.
"All this searching is making me hungry," said Bear.
"Maybe Josie's having lunch?" asked Mouse.

But she wasn't.
"We'll catch up with you," said Bear.
"Mm-hmm," mumbled Mouse.

Every time they thought they saw her,
it turned out to be a mistake. And worse,
Bunny's friends kept getting distracted.

Raccoon crept into the computer room.

Frog leapt into the water fountain.

Mole dug into the science lab.

And still, there was no sign of Josie.

"Looks like it's just you and me, Porcupine," sighed
Bunny. "Porcupine?"

But Bunny was too late. Porcupine had dipped into
the art room, and now he was stuck.

"I suppose one friend is better than none," said Bunny sadly.
He continued down the corridor. And that's when he saw it.
Bunny's heart hopped.

He burst into the school's library. It smelled like home!
He spotted his favorite book. Then another. And
another! There were new stories, too, just waiting to be
read. Bunny gleefully ran his paws across them all . . .

. . . then paused at the end of the shelves.

Just then, Porcupine, Bird, Frog, Bear, Mouse, Mole, Raccoon, and Squirrel toppled into the library.

"We knew we'd find you here!" said Porcupine.

"It's Josie!" shouted Bunny, pointing to
the playground. "Look!"

Bear held open the back door. The animals ran out and
dashed to the jungle gym. They caused quite a kerfuffle!
Which caused Josie to look up.

And smile.

She hugged her friends.
They hugged her right back.

"Wanna play?" asked Josie.
"You bet!" said Bunny.

Soon everyone joined in the fun. (Bear caused a bit of a delay.)

They raced and chased all around until recess was over.

Before heading back inside, Josie grabbed Bunny's paw.
"Thank you," she whispered.
Bunny beamed.

Josie lined up with her class. "See you
Saturday!" she called.
Bunny waved goodbye. He could see Josie
had made lots of new friends.

And so had he.